Sunk!

For Daniel and Amanda

HarperCollins
PUBLISHERS
Since 1817

First published in hardback in Great Britain by HarperCollins Children's Books in 2017
First published in paperback in 2017
HarperCollins Children's Books is a division of HarperCollins Publishers Ltd.
Text and illustrations copyright © Rob Biddulph 2017

Visit our website at www.harpercollins.co.uk

ISBN: 978-0-00-820740-3
Printed and bound in China
1 3 5 7 9 10 8 6 4 2

Written and illustrated by

RobBiddulph

HarperCollins *Children's Books*

A pirate hat.
A sunny day.
For Penguin Blue
a game to play.

With Cutlass Jeff

and First Mate Flo.

"Avast me hearties!
Yo ho ho!"

A pirate penguin needs a ship.
Here's Clive, back from his fishing trip.

"Eyes starboard Cap'n.
Friend ahoy!"

Meet Wilbur Seal
– the cabin boy.

"Hoist the colours!"
"Set the sail!"

It's time to hit the treasure trail!

And sail across...

the seven seas...

Then suddenly...
Oh no! A rip!

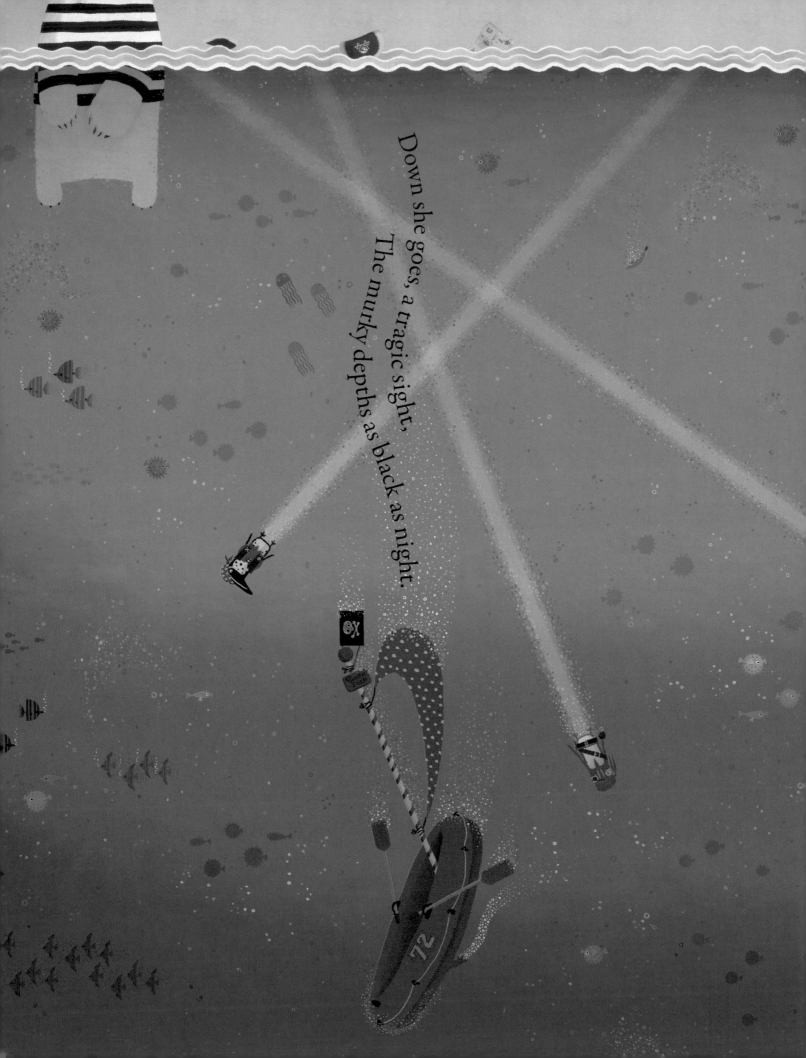

Down she goes, a tragic sight,
The murky depths as black as night.

But wait. A flag...

A mast...

A deck...

Well blow me down,
a sunken wreck!

NEPTUNE'S DREAD

For Penguin Blue a closer look.
"I know this ship. It's in my book."
The once majestic *Neptune's Dread*
sleeps silent on the ocean bed.

Alas, there's no time to explore.
Tired penguins need to get ashore.

A desert island, small and sandy.
Phew! That is *extremely* handy.

"Look!" says Flo,
"There's someone waving."

"Help me!
I'm in need
of saving!"

"My name is Captain Walker Plank.
Been stuck here since my galleon sank."

"The famous Plank!" says Penguin Blue.
"It's such a thrill to rescue you!"

"Why thanks swashbucklers,
but, worse luck...

...I think that you are also stuck!"

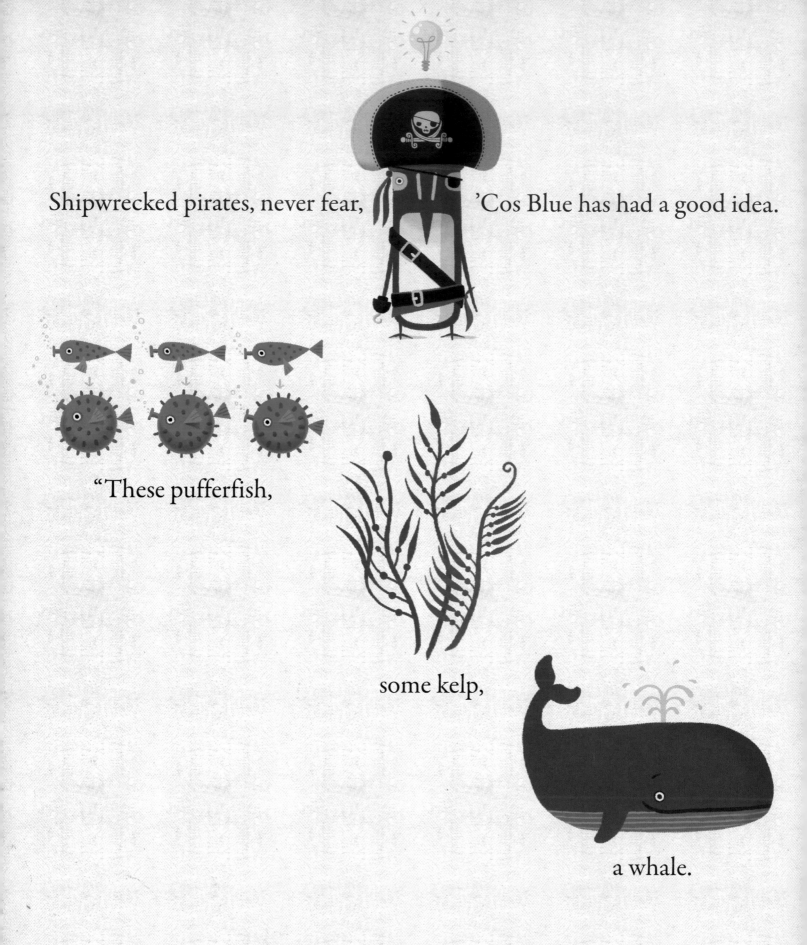

Shipwrecked pirates, never fear,   'Cos Blue has had a good idea.

"These pufferfish,

some kelp,

a whale.

We'll raise the ship and home we'll sail."

The fish inflate and up she goes,
towards the surface...

..."THAR SHE BLOWS!"

"My ship!" cries Plank,
"We're saved! Three cheers!
All aboard, brave buccaneers!"

Through swollen waves
and dancing foam

The grateful Captain
tows them home.

Two pirate hats.
A sunny day.
For Penguin Blue
a friend to stay.

Fun times with
buddies, new and old.

That's treasure worth
much more than gold.